The Princess and the Spider

A pattern woven from silvery strands stretched from tree to tree. Stuck in the middle of the pattern was a fat bear, struggling to get out. But the more he struggled, the more he became entangled in the thick, sticky threads. "Help me!" he cried when he saw Willie. "Oh please, help me."

The disguised princess took a step forward. "Is that a spiderweb?" she asked nervously.

"It sure is," moaned the bear. "And if I don't get out of it soon, I'll be spider food. Please, cut me down!"

Willie drew her sword and started toward the web. She was so intent on what she was doing that she didn't see the huge black spider that stepped into the clearing from the other side. . . .

✳ ✳ ✳

THE DRAGONSLAYERS is on the 1997 Master List for the Pacific Northwest Young Reader's Choice Award

Books by Bruce Coville:

Available from Simon & Schuster

THE DRAGONSLAYERS

BRUCE COVILLE

Illustrated by Katherine Coville

Aladdin Paperbacks

New York London Toronto Sydney Singapore

For the students and staff of
Wetzel Road Elementary School

First Aladdin Paperbacks edition January 2002
Originally published by Minstrel Books in July 1994

ALADDIN PAPERBACKS
An imprint of Simon & Schuster
Children's Publishing Division
1230 Avenue of the Americas
New York, NY 10020

Manufactured in the United States of America
20 19

ISBN-13: 978-0-671-79832-1
ISBN-10: 0-671-79832-4
0212 OFF

1

Making a Dragon

"Do you have the lizard snot?" asked Grizelda.

"Right here," said Phrenella, holding up a tiny green bottle.

Midnight thunder rumbled in the distance as Grizelda rubbed her hands together with delight. "Good," she cackled. "We're ready to begin!"

The two witches were standing in front of Grizelda's cottage—a thatch-roofed dwelling hidden deep in the Forest of Wonder. Golden leaves were falling all around them. Between the witches, suspended above a low-burning fire, was a huge black cauldron filled with a bubbling brew. A dozen or so goons, the strange, green-skinned creatures who did

1

Grizelda's bidding, lurked at the edges of the clearing.

"Let the conjuring commence!" cried Grizelda. Rolling up her sleeves, she began to wave her skinny arms over the cauldron.

"Goons, bring your ingredients!" ordered Phrenella.

As the goons lumbered forward with the things Grizelda had sent them to gather, she began to chant strange and incomprehensible words. One by one, the goons tossed their treasures into the bubbling cauldron. The fire made their shadows flicker and dance around the edge of the clearing.

The wind began to pick up. The storm was getting closer.

Phrenella stood near the fire, muttering the names of the things the goons tossed into the cauldron, as if checking them against a list. "Moondust and mildew; toad tongues, bat wings, fireflowers and wormwood . . ." These were just the beginning of the list. Soon there were other things, things too strange and fierce to mention.

The cauldron began to boil more fiercely. A smell of fear and sulphur rose from the strange brew.

"No eye of newt?" asked Phrenella at last.

"Eye?" cried Grizelda. "What eye? I'm using the whole thing!"

With that she pulled a tiny lizard from her pocket. "Behold!" she cried, pointing to the squirming creature. "The dragon-to-be!"

With that, she hurled the newt into the cauldron. Raising her arms above her head, she began a new chant, her words low and menacing at first, then growing steadily louder until finally she was shrieking her incantation:

3

"Powers of the deep and dark,
Grizelda calls! Send me your spark—
Use my hate to fuel this fire;
Let it work my heart's desire.
Let King lose child, as I lost mine,
Let him drink revenge's bitter wine.
Raise the dragon, raise him now,
To fill Grizelda's hate-born vow!"

Suddenly the storm broke. Grizelda erupted in wild laughter as bolts of lightning streaked through the jet-black sky, sending the goons scurrying for shelter. Thunder seemed to shake the trees where they stood. A shaft of lightning sizzled into the very center of the clearing—into the cauldron itself.

With a tremendous explosion the cauldron flew into thousands of pieces. For a moment all was silent. Then a tiny creature—something like a lizard, yet somehow . . . different—scrambled from the wreckage. Rearing on its hind legs, it spit fire at one of the goons, which ran shrieking into the forest as flames singed its pants.

The tiny dragon gave a piercing cry, then turned and raced in the other direction. Soon it had disappeared among the trees.

"He not very big," said one of the goons, sounding puzzled.

"Oh, he'll grow," cackled Grizelda. "He'll grow. By spring he'll be—remarkable!"

Grabbing her broom, she leapt astride it and soared into the darkness. Her shrieks of laughter seemed to hang in the air behind her as she vanished in the wild October sky.

2

Disorder in the Court

"No, no, no! I won't do it!"

The speaker was the Princess Wilhelmina—known as Willie for short, since she was the most willful person anyone in the kingdom had ever met.

"Of course you'll do it," said her father, King Mildred.

(King Mildred had never gotten over his unfortunate name, which had caused him no end of trouble when he was a boy. As far as he was concerned, he had been so much kinder in naming his daughter than his parents had been to him that a simple matter such as whom she would marry—or whether she would marry at all—should have been no problem.)

"I will not!" shouted Willie. She crossed

her arms and shook her head, causing her long red hair to slide back and forth over her shoulders.

"Why?" asked her mother, Queen Hortense. "That's what I don't understand, Willie. I would think you would be delighted that your father is ready to choose your husband. The suitors *are* getting anxious, dear."

"Have you seen them, Mother?" cried Willie. "One is old, one is fat, and one is ugly."

"And they're all willing to marry you— which is no small thing, considering how pigheaded you are," said King Mildred.

"You're the one who's being pigheaded, Father!" cried Willie. "Why do I have to get married at all?"

"Wilhelmina!" cried the queen in shock. "You're fourteen years old. You don't want to wither on the vine, do you?"

"No, but I want to be ripe before I get plucked!"

Her mother sighed. "You need a husband to take care of you, dear, to—"

"Oh, don't be silly, Mother," interrupted Willie. "I can take care of myself. I wouldn't mind getting married someday—*if* I fell in love. But there's a lot I want to do first."

7

"Oh, really?" asked the king, raising one bushy gray eyebrow. "Care to give us an example?"

Willie's eyes lit with excitement. "Well, I want to learn to ride a horse . . . and use a sword. I want to see the world. I want to have adventures. But most of all," she cried, so excited that she leapt from her chair, *"I want to be a knight!"*

A gasp of horror rose from the assembled lords. They had been ignoring the argument up to this point; they were more than used to Willie arguing with her parents. But this was beyond anything they had ever heard. One of the maids-in-waiting fainted with embarrassment.

"Willie!" hissed the king. "You mustn't talk that way!"

"Why not?" asked Wilhelmina, genuinely puzzled.

"Because you're a young lady, dear," explained the queen with a sigh. "No real young lady would even think of such things."

"It's just not fair!" shouted Wilhelmina, stamping her foot again.

"What's not fair?" asked the king.

"The boys get everything that's interesting. *They* get horses. What do I get? Kittens! They

8

get helmets. What do I get? Hairpins! They get swords. What do I get? *Embroidery needles!*"

The page boys smiled and nodded. This was the way it had always been, and as far as they were concerned, it made perfect sense.

"Willie, that's enough," snapped the king. "You are a princess, and a princess can't—"

His words were cut off by a cry from the huge doors at the front of the throne room. "Horror and woe!" wailed the voice. "Death and destruction. Horror and woe! Monstrous! Monstrous!"

"What's going on there?" cried the king. "Guards, go see to it. Willie, sit down. You boys straighten out, too," he added, gesturing to the pages, who had started giggling and making jokes among themselves.

Everyone turned to the great doors at the front of the room. Two guards marched in, carrying between them a peasant woman dressed in smoking, tattered rags.

"Here she is, Your Majesty," said the first guard. "The one who was making all that squawking."

"She insisted on seeing you," added the second.

"Good Lord, woman!" cried King Mildred. "What happened?"

"It was awful!" cried the peasant. Though her eyes were wide, she appeared to be looking at something far from the courtroom.

"What was awful?" asked the king.

"You're right," said the woman, turning slowly toward him. "It *was!*"

"What are you talking about?" bellowed the king.

"The dragon!" cried the peasant woman.

Then she fell over in a dead faint.

3

The King's Promise

"WELL," SAID WILLIE, PUSHING UP HER SLEEVES AND climbing off her throne. "This is getting interesting!"

"Wilhelmina, be quiet!" snapped the queen. "Don't you know that dragons love fried princess more than anything?"

"Oh, yeah?" cried Willie. "Well, let him try me. I'll pull his teeth out. I'll knock his—"

"Hush, Willie!" snapped the king, waving a hand in her direction. He turned back to the peasant woman. Several of the maids-in-waiting had rushed to her side and were helping her to a sitting position. One was fanning her face, another lightly slapping her cheeks.

"Now, what is this all about?" asked King Mildred.

"A dragon from the Forest of Wonder is ravaging the kingdom!" cried the peasant. "A fierce, man-eating, house-burning dragon! He's eight feet tall and twenty feet long. He has a face made of fear, teeth like daggers, a roar that can stop your heart."

"Well, what do you want me to do about it?" asked the king, looking confused.

"Send a knight to kill the thing!"

The king sank back in his chair with a groan.

"I'll do it!" cried Willie, jumping to her feet.

Grabbing Willie by the shoulder, Queen Hortense pulled her back into her chair.

"One of you pages go fetch the knights," said King Mildred with a wave of his hand. "Tell them I want them here right away."

"I'll go!" cried a dark-haired boy, the shortest of the lot.

The king nodded and said, "Thank you, Brian."

The other pages sighed and made faces at Brian as he left the room.

While waiting for his knights, King Mildred sent the peasant woman to be cared for by a doctor, told Wilhelmina that she would have to pick a husband by morning, and tried to get

13

the court to settle down. Willie was winding up to argue with him again when the knights came parading in.

The king pinched the bridge of his nose and shook his head. He only had three knights, and they were the shame of the kingdom, a bumbling collection of fools and clowns that could be counted on to embarrass him in important situations.

"You called, Your Majesty?" asked Sir Pentamon, the leader of the group.

"Yes, I called," said the king. "I want you to—"

"Dungeon dust!" cried Sir Wexler, the last knight in the line. "I forgot my sword. Go get it, Elizar!"

"Yes, sir! At once, sir!" said a tall, skinny man who had come trailing in behind the knights. He had a bald head and a long gray beard, and he had endured a brief bout of fame the year before when someone had discovered that he was the world's oldest working squire.

"You were saying, Your Highness?" asked Sir Pentamon as Elizar went running out.

The king cleared his throat. "I have a small job for one of you men."

Sir Filibuster, the second most senior knight, grinned broadly. "Small jobs are our specialty."

"I know," replied the king sharply. "How-

14

ever, this one is a tiny bit larger than usual. I want one of you to go slay a dragon."

Sir Pentamon blinked in astonishment. "A *dragon?*" he squeaked. Then, lowering his voice, he repeated: "A dragon?"

"Yes," said the king, "a dragon. As I said, it's a small job—the sort of thing you expect every day from a knight."

He decided not to mention that since the kingdom had had an unusually long stretch of good luck and peace, none of his own knights were used to this sort of thing.

"Well, I would do it myself, Your Highness," said Sir Pentamon, "but as you probably recall, I have been having a lot of trouble with my back lately. . . ."

Willie snorted, causing Sir Pentamon to glare at her.

The king turned his attention to Sir Filibuster, who looked like a man who had just been told he was going to have his teeth pulled out one by one. "Sorry, Your Highness," he muttered. "I dislocated my shoulder during jousting practice last week. Couldn't consider it for at least another month."

The king growled and turned his attention to Sir Wexler.

"Love to, sire!" he cried. "But couldn't possibly, not this week. Armor's leaking, don't you know. A little rain and I'd fill right up. Dragon would make a teakettle out of me in nothing flat."

By now the king was red with rage. "Isn't there one of you who will take on this task?" he roared.

The knights began busily examining their fingernails.

"Not one?" cried the king. "Oh, what a crew of fools and cowards! I'd give half my kingdom for a knight with some courage!"

He stopped, as if realizing what he had just said, then pounded the arm of his throne. "I will! Half my kingdom to whoever slays that dragon!"

"Mildred!" gasped the queen in dismay. But she had nothing to worry about. The knights simply stared at the floor and muttered.

The king was so angry he began to shake. Then his eyes widened as he spotted a way to kill two birds with one stone. "My daughter's hand in marriage to whoever slays that dragon!" he thundered.

"Father!" shrieked Wilhelmina, jumping to her feet.

At that moment Elizar came running into the throne room with Sir Wexler's sword. "Here I am!" he shouted, heading for the knights.

"Who said that?" cried the king.

"He did!" replied the knights with one voice, turning and pointing at Elizar.

The king smiled. "Thank you, my good man," he said cheerfully.

"You're welcome, sire," replied Elizar, nodding and smiling back. After a second he added, "For what?"

"For being the only one in this crew of ninnies with the courage to face that dragon!"

Elizar stared at the king in astonishment. Suddenly his eyes rolled back in his head and his knees buckled.

The knights managed to catch him before he hit the floor.

"He's overwhelmed, Your Highness," said Sir Pentamon.

"He's wanted a chance like this for years," added Sir Filibuster.

"He's as happy about it as you are!" added Sir Wexler, who was patting Elizar's face, trying to rouse him. "As happy as we are, almost."

Elizar's eyes fluttered open. As he looked at

the knights surrounding him, a strange expression crossed his wrinkled face. Struggling to his feet, he drew himself to his full height—which was considerable—and said, "That is right. It is an honor to serve my king in any way. I thank you for this wonderful chance, Your Highness."

Sir Pentamon began to blink. Sir Filibuster made a sour face. Sir Wexler's eyes bulged in astonishment.

"You are most welcome, Elizar," said the king with a nod. "Tell me, is there any way we can help you in your quest?"

Elizar thought for a moment, then said, "Well, a sword and a shield might be useful."

"Of course, of course," said the king. "Take your pick from the armory."

"And then—well, I'm the only squire in the castle, sire. If I am to act as a knight . . ." He paused, embarrassed at having to say it.

"Go ahead," urged the king. "What is it?"

"Well, I'll need a squire myself."

"I'll do it!" cried Brian.

The other page boys stared at him in a way that indicated they would be perfectly happy if the dragon managed to swallow him whole at some point during the adventure. But King Mil-

dred nodded and said, "You shall be Elizar's squire, Brian. Serve him well on this great quest."

"I will, Your Majesty," said Brian, making a deep bow.

King Mildred raised his hand and said, "I pronounce you—the Dragonslayers! Now go forth and slay this mighty beast."

He didn't notice the look on his daughter's face, nor hear her mutter to herself, "Not if I get there first, Daddy."

4

Flipping the Page

AN HOUR LATER BRIAN ENTERED THE ROOM HE shared with the other pages. Georg, the tallest of the group, was waiting for him at the door. "Well, you did it again!" he said as Brian came in. He gave Brian a shove, adding, "You are such a clod. I just can't believe you."

"Hey!" cried Brian. He stumbled backward, falling over Farrell, the skinniest of the group, who had knelt behind him.

"Don't be so surprised, Georg," said Edric, who was the widest of the pages. He plunked himself down on Brian's chest. "It's always the same. Here's a job—there's Brian, just panting to do it. What a bonehead."

"Thanks again, Brian Bootlicker," snarled

Farrell. Scrambling to his feet, he kicked Brian in the side. "We all love looking like cowards."

"You could have volunteered!" gasped Brian. He was having a hard time breathing with Edric on top of him. He squirmed, trying to break free, but it was no use.

"Volunteer to get eaten by the dragon?" cried Georg, giving him a kick from the other side. "How stupid do you think we are?"

Brian shook his head. "I don't understand," he said, fighting back tears. "If you don't want the job, why do you care if I do it?"

"Because you get so much pleasure out of making us look bad!" said Edric as Farrell and Georg attacked again, harder than ever.

"Stop it!" cried Brian, struggling to throw Edric off. "Stop! Leave me alone!"

"We'll leave you alone all right," sneered Farrell. "Alone with that old loon, Elizar."

"Uh-oh!" cried Velton, who had been set outside the room to watch. "Someone's coming. Let's get out of here."

Edric scrambled off Brian. Laughing, the pages raced out of the room. Georg, the last to leave, turned and shouted, "So long—*hero!*"

Brian lay on the floor for a moment, trying to stop the flow of tears.

"I'll show you!" he shouted when he had his breath back, even though he knew the others were gone. "I'll show you . . . ," he repeated, this time in little more than a whisper.

He rolled over and pushed himself to his knees, then climbed to his feet. "I hate those creeps," he muttered as he limped to the small trunk where he kept his things. He opened the lid. But instead of reaching inside, he leaned his head against the wood and whispered, "I don't get it. What's so bad about wanting to do something good?"

A clank at the door drew his attention. Turning his head, he saw Elizar standing in the archway. The old man was dressed in ill-fitting armor and holding a rusty sword as if he wasn't quite sure what to do with it. He started to say something, but was interrupted by the visor of his helmet clanking down in front of his face. Little bits of his beard stuck through the vents in the metal.

"I heard some of that," he said, struggling to lift the visor.

"It was nothing new," muttered Brian.

"Of course it's not new," replied Elizar, finally getting his visor back in place. "The world has always had more than enough lazy yahoos. Doesn't make them right, just—plentiful."

The boy looked at the old man. With his ramshackle armor and battered shield, he was hardly the kind of knight Brian himself dreamed of becoming. Yet it was Elizar who had found the courage to take on a task that the other knights, the real knights, were too frightened to accept.

"Do you think we actually have a chance against the dragon?" Brian whispered.

Elizar shrugged, causing a series of loud clanks. "I believe there's always a chance."

Brian looked past Elizar, down the hall where the other pages had disappeared. "But they all think . . ."

Elizar frowned. "You are my squire. Tell me what *you* think."

Brian paused, then smiled and said, "I think this is the adventure I've been waiting for all my life!"

Elizar smiled back. "Shall we go slay a dragon?" he asked, holding out his hand.

Brian took the outstretched hand and clasped it in his own. "Let's do it!"

To Brian's surprise, they didn't head straight for the castle gate. Instead, Elizar took him to the armory. "You should have a sword and a shield of your own," said the old man. "After all, you never know what might happen on a mission like this."

Unfortunately, the swords Brian liked best were all too big for him. Finally he settled for a smaller sword, which he named Dragon-whacker. Even though its leather scabbard was a trifle shabby, the feel of it at his side delighted him as he followed Elizar across the drawbridge of King Mildred's castle.

They saw the Forest of Wonder long before they entered it—a great looming presence that seemed as if it could hold all manner of strange and terrible things.

"I've heard stories about this place since I was little," Brian whispered as they drew closer to its borders.

Elizar nodded. Everyone in the kingdom had heard the old tales of talking animals and half-human creatures that dwelt in the Forest of Wonder. They had heard rumors, too, of the odd enchantments that might befall unwary travelers who crossed the forest's border.

It was nearly dusk when they reached the first of the great trees. Other trees stretched to the sides and into the distance as far as they could see—which was not far, given the thick undergrowth. Streamers of moss and thick vines trailed from the branches.

Moving warily, the two adventurers followed a path that wound past trees wider than Brian was tall. Now and then they heard strange rustlings among the new spring leaves. But try as they might, they were never able to see what caused the sounds.

When night fell they camped beside a small stream, where the water gurgled around rocks and splashed down tiny falls.

"According to what the peasant woman told me, we should go this way," said Elizar the next morning, clanking over the stepping-stones that led across the stream.

It was another day before they saw their first sign of the dragon. They had just passed a large cave and were entering a clearing when Brian spotted a black strip that stretched for at least thirty feet along the ground. He stooped to examine it. When he ran his fingertips over the surface they came away black and sooty.

"Elizar," he muttered nervously, "is this what I think it is?"

"If you're thinking it's a scorch mark, I'd say

yes," replied the old knight. He lifted his visor, which had fallen over his eyes again, and squinted at the black strip. "I don't see what else it could be."

"But it's so *long!*" whispered Brian.

Elizar nodded, catching his visor just in time. "Must be a big dragon," he said quietly.

Brian looked up at him. "Did you ever kill a dragon?"

Elizar laughed. "Of course not! Until two days ago I was only a squire. Besides, we haven't had a dragon around here for over a hundred years." He paused, then added proudly, "I did read a book about it once!"

"And I've dreamed about it," said Brian. He sighed. "What a pair we are."

"We'll do," said Elizar.

"Since no one else will even try, I guess we'll have to," replied Brian. Still studying the scorch mark, he asked, "How come you're not a knight anyway, Elizar? You're worth more than that batch of ninnies at court all put together."

The old man smiled sadly. "I was never trained for it, Brian. The truth is, I was just an old-fashioned peasant until the day the king dragged me off to war. When I came back, I found that my cottage had been burned to the ground." He paused. When he continued his voice was thick with pain. "My wife and child were gone. For months I wandered aimlessly, cursing the fates and the enemy that had burned my home. Finally I ended up at King Mildred's castle. They happened to be looking for a squire, and having nothing else to do, I volunteered for the job. I've worked there ever since."

Brian tightened his mouth. An orphan himself, he found the old man's story stirring up feelings of loss and hurt that he usually kept pressed deep inside him. "I'm sorry, Elizar," he whispered. "I didn't . . ."

Elizar shook his head. "That was many years ago. Come on, we'd better get moving."

They hadn't gone more than fifteen paces when Brian stopped and said, "What's that?"

"Sounds like someone calling for help," said Elizar after a moment.

"That's what I thought!" Brian replied eagerly. "Well, we'll have to go to his aid. It's our knightly duty."

With a sigh Elizar hitched up his sword. But before he had time to take another step, the trouble came to them.

5

Willie Steps Out

WILLIE WAS FUMING AS SHE STOMPED UP THE STAIRS to her room. "I can't believe my father," she muttered. "First he says that whoever slays the dragon can marry me—and then he sends Elizar off to do it. *Elizar!* The man is old enough to be my father himself. My grandfather, for heaven's sake!"

She slammed her door, then threw herself across her bed, which was covered by a pink satin spread that she had always found particularly revolting.

"*I* could have done it," she said, rolling over and throttling an embroidered pillow. "Why didn't he send me?"

Throwing aside the pillow, she jumped from the bed and went to the large chair near her window. Arranging herself in her father's favorite position—hand on knee, chin in hand—she furrowed her brow and put on a slightly worried expression. Imitating his voice, she answered her own question: "Because you're a girl, dear."

With a growl she jumped up and went back to sit on her bed. "So?" she asked.

She ran back to the chair.

"Not only that, you are the only heir to the throne. We can't take any chances with you."

Scooting back to the bed, she looked at the chair and said sweetly, "Didn't *you* take chances before you became king, Daddy?"

Back to the chair: "Yes, but that was different."

Back to the bed: "Why?"

Back to the chair: "Because *I* was a boy!"

She closed her eyes for a moment, then jumped up and shouted, "AAARGH!"

Now, usually when a princess "aaarghs" like that, someone comes running to help her. However, people in King Mildred's castle had long ago learned that when Willie "aaarghed" it was best to leave her alone.

"Well, I've had enough of that nonsense," she said. She climbed onto her bed and started to bounce—an action that revealed the army boots she secretly wore under her dress.

"I've been waiting [bounce] for a chance [bounce] to prove [bounce] what I can do. [Bounce, bounce.] I'm not [bounce] going to let [bounce] it get past [bounce] me now!"

She bounced again, higher than ever, then stretched herself out so that she landed flat on the bed.

"Oh, who am I kidding?" she moaned after she had stopped flopping up and down. "I've said that a hundred times, and here I stay, pretty as a picture—and just about as active."

At that moment one of the maids-in-waiting poked her head into the room. "Come on, Willie!" she called. "We're going to embroider a banner for the Dragonslayers!"

"Embroider?" bellowed Willie. "A banner? While those guys go off to slay the dragon? Not me. Listen—life's out there calling. Can't you hear it?"

The maid tipped her head to one side and listened. She closed her eyes and tried harder. Finally she shook her head and said, "I can't hear a thing."

"Oh, you're hopeless!" cried Willie, flinging a pillow at her. "Go on! Go!"

Blinking in astonishment, the maid turned and ran.

"A banner," muttered Willie in disgust. "That does it. I'm going after that dragon myself!"

She looked down at her elegant pink dress and snorted in disgust. "I sure can't do it dressed like this, though! Gad, I wish my parents thought my insides were as important as my outsides! I'm so sick of this frilly stuff I could scream."

She began taking off her dress, which had over forty buttons. Deciding that the regular method was too slow, she ripped it open instead. Buttons flew in all directions.

"So much for that," she said, throwing the dress onto the bed. "And for these, too," she added, tossing seven rings, three bracelets, and a necklace on top of it. "They'll only attract attention."

Once she had torn off several layers of lacy undergarments, she hurried to the huge wardrobe that stood against the far wall. Twice as tall as she was, it was carved all over with unicorns and gryphons. Flinging open the door on the right, Willie began digging around in the mess inside.

(The wardrobe had not always been a mess inside, but Willie had long ago trained the woman in charge of cleaning her room not to touch what was in there. It hadn't been easy, but Willie had prevailed.)

After a few minutes she surfaced with some worn and patched clothing—a pair of trousers, an old shirt, a vest, and a wide-brimmed hat.

"I've had this stuff for nearly a year and never dared to use it," she muttered as she pulled on the disguise. "Well, the time has come. Let's see how it looks."

She turned a panel of the wardrobe, revealing a full-length mirror.

"Not bad," she said, pivoting and glancing over her shoulder. She pinned up her coppery hair, then tucked it under her hat. She looked again, expecting to see a reflection that could be taken for that of a peasant boy. But after examining herself for a moment, she moaned in despair.

"No one's going to believe this," she said. "Look at that skin. Peaches and cream, Mother always calls it. It's so wholesome it's revolting! I'll have to do something about that if I want to fool anyone."

It wasn't easy to find dirt in her room, which was kept dinner-plate clean by the palace staff. She finally had to shove her bed away from the wall to locate some. After smearing it on her forehead and one cheek, she returned to the mirror.

"Much better!" she said happily. "Far more urchinlike. Now for the final touch."

Returning to her bed, she dug between mattresses number six and number seven, where she had hidden a sword that she had sneaked from the castle armory several months earlier. Holding it aloft, she smiled and said, "That dragon had better watch out now!"

Suddenly she heard footsteps coming down the hall. Quickly she returned to the wardrobe. She opened another drawer, reached inside, and pushed a secret button.

Swiftly and silently the back of the wardrobe slid open.

"You must never use this unless your life is in danger," Queen Hortense had said when she first showed Willie the door. "It is only for the most desperate of emergencies."

"I'm sure this qualifies," muttered Willie as she stepped into the passage, "since I know I'll die if I have to marry Elizar."

Pulling the door shut behind her, she leaned her head against it and whispered, "So long, Mom and Dad. I'm off to slay a dragon!"

She took a deep breath. Then she turned and ran silently down the dark passage, out of the castle and into the world.

6

Goons

BRIAN AND ELIZAR WATCHED IN ASTONISHMENT AS a pair of Grizelda's goons stepped into the clearing. The creatures were dragging a large fox between them. When the fox spotted the two humans it cried, "Help! Hellllllp! You have to save me!"

Brian blinked in surprise, until he remembered that talking animals were not considered unusual in the Forest of Wonder.

Elizar began waving his sword. "Drop that fox!" he cried, struggling to lift his visor.

The first goon, which was much shorter than Elizar, but also considerably wider and more muscular, sneered and said, "Move aside, old man!"

Brian stepped up beside Elizar and shouted, "He told you to drop the fox!"

To his surprise, the goons did drop the fox. It raced off among the trees, yelping as it went. But rather than running off themselves, the goons began to make threatening faces at Brian and Elizar. Glaring wickedly, they hooted and scratched under their armpits, jumping up and down in a strange dance. Then they separated and began to move in a circle around the two.

"Stand ready, Brian," whispered Elizar.

"I'm at your side," replied the page boy.

Suddenly the goons charged, waving their arms and screaming.

"Back to back!" whispered Elizar.

Brian swiveled so that his back was to Elizar's. They drew their swords and began to wave them in the air. As the goons darted in, hissing and clawing, Brian felt a surge of fear ripple through him. It was unlike anything he had ever experienced before. He would have turned to run, but Elizar was right behind him.

In terror he ran forward instead. This unexpected action so startled the goon facing him that it screamed and began backing away.

"Grizelda!" it shrieked. "Grizelda!"

The fear was catching. In an instant the other goon was backing away, too. When Elizar yelled, both goons went racing into the forest.

Elizar stared after them for a moment. Then he clapped Brian on the shoulder. "Well done, my boy! It was your brave charge that turned the trick."

Brian blushed, wondering if he should tell Elizar the truth about how afraid he had been. Just as he was deciding that it was the only honorable thing to do, the fox came creeping from behind one of the trees. "Thank goodness you were here!" it said. "No telling what those things might have done to me if you hadn't come along."

"What were they?" asked Elizar uneasily.

"Goons," said the fox. "They work for Grizelda."

"Grizelda?" asked Brian.

"She's the chief witch in these parts," said the fox, licking a paw. "They caught me spying on her. I wasn't, really. I was just . . . listening. They were talking about the dragon."

Brian smiled. "The dragon, huh? Well, we'll take care of *that* problem."

The fox looked as astonished as Brian had felt when he first heard the animal speak. "What are you talking about?" it asked.

"Just what I said," replied Brian. "We're here to kill the dragon.

The fox made a little bark of amusement. "I'm not sure it *can* be killed—at least, not in the usual way." It glanced from side to side, as if to be sure that no one else was listening, then whispered, "Grizelda *made* him, you know."

The visor on Elizar's helmet fell down with a clang. "This witch *made* the dragon?" he asked, struggling to get the helmet open again.

"That's what I heard the goons say," replied the fox. It glanced from side to side again, then whispered, "I was spying on them. At least, I was until they caught me."

"Well, magic or not, it's our job to kill the thing," said Brian. He pulled Dragonwhacker from its sheath and began waving it at the bushes, as if the dragon might be lurking somewhere nearby.

The fox tilted its head to one side and watched. "Mind if I come along?" it asked, after a moment.

"Why would you want to do that?" asked Elizar, finally managing to pry open his helmet.

The fox smiled. "Let's just say I have a fondness for hopeless causes. Besides, last week the dragon burned down one of my favorite trees. I'd love to help get rid of him."

"I don't know. . . ." said Elizar.

"Never turn away a friend," said the fox.

Elizar looked at Brian. Brian looked at the fox.

"I'm a good tracker," it said. "Got a nose as sharp as a hawk's eye."

Brian shrugged. "Sounds good to me. Come on, we'd better get—"

His words were interrupted by a distant roar.

"It's *him!*" whispered the fox.

"Let's go!" cried Brian eagerly. He led the way from the clearing. The fox came next. Elizar, who found it hard to move in his armor, came clanking along behind.

So intent were they on pursuing the dragon that they did not notice the eyes that watched them as they left. Nor did they hear the chuckle of the goon that had been spying on them as it scampered off to report to Grizelda.

7

Spider

Soon after the spying goon left in search of Grizelda, Princess Wilhelmina entered the same clearing. She had her eyes fixed on the ground. A moment later she knelt to examine something.

"Looks like Brian and Elizar were in a fight," she muttered to herself. "I wonder who it was with."

She continued to study the ground, trying to remember everything she had learned about tracking from her father's library. After a moment she spotted a trail leading out of the clearing. Recognizing the mark of Elizar's boots, she smiled. Even though she needed to beat her rivals to the dragon, she was glad they had survived the fight.

Remembering a tip from one of the books, she pressed her finger against some of the overturned soil.

It was still moist.

"Good," she said, pushing back her hat. "It's fairly fresh. Which means they can't be far ahead of me. If I can manage to circle around them, maybe I can get to the dragon first. Now, let's see . . ."

She gazed into the forest, trying to decide the best way to flank Brian and Elizar. But before she could make up her mind, she heard a distant voice cry, "Help! Someone help me!"

She scrambled to her feet and looked around. Then she held very still and listened once more.

"Help! *Help!*"

Willie hesitated for a moment. She didn't want to take time away from her quest. But she knew that if she wanted to be a knight, she had to answer any call for help—even if it meant putting off her own business. With a sigh she began running through the trees. She stopped once, waiting until she heard the voice again.

"That way!" she murmured.

She splashed across a stream, then scrambled up a steep slope. She stopped again at the edge of a clearing. This was where the screams were coming from.

Eyes wide, heart pounding, she peered through a curtain of new spring leaves.

She gasped in horror.

An enormous spiderweb stretched across the center of the clearing. Its intricate pattern was woven from silvery strands as thick as her little finger. Stuck in the middle of the web was a fat bear. It was struggling desperately to get out, but the more it tugged and pulled, the more it became entangled in the thick, sticky threads.

"Help me!" it cried when it saw Willie. "Please, help me!"

The disguised princess took a step forward. "Is that a spiderweb?" she asked. Her throat felt dry, and it was hard to get the words out.

"It sure is," moaned the bear. "And if I don't get out of it soon, I'll be spider *food*. Please, cut me down!"

Willie drew her sword and began moving toward the web. She was so intent on what she was doing that she didn't see the enormous black spider that stepped into the clearing from the other side.

The spider, however, saw her. Rubbing together two of its eight legs, it hissed, "My, my, my. Supper *and* dessert! Better put the sword away, little boy. You might get hurt."

"You let that bear go!" said Willie, backing away from the spider.

"Never!" hissed the spider as it started toward her. Its spindly legs held it so high above the ground it could stare Willie straight in the eye. Its head was the size of a melon. The body that swelled behind the head was several times larger still.

Willie found herself staring into eyes as big as her fists. They seemed to have as many facets as the best diamonds in her father's treasury. So many facets, all of them sparkling, sparkling . . .

"Hey, boy!" cried the bear desperately. "Wake up!"

Willie blinked, and realized that the spider had actually started to wrap her in its thread. Screaming with rage, she lashed out with her sword and cut the strands that held her legs. As she did, her sword slashed into the spider's side.

With a bloodcurdling scream it jumped away, twisting to look at its wound.

"Kill her!" urged the bear. "Now!"

"Not while her back is turned," said Willie grimly, raising her sword once more.

"How gallant," hissed the spider, turning to face Willie again. "And how foolish!"

Now Willie did lunge forward. But the spider leapt backward, moving easily out of her reach. Turning, it scrambled up a tree. Then it hurled itself into the air. A thick strand of thread stretched behind it as it hurtled toward Willie, who threw herself to the ground and rolled away.

She lay on her stomach, as if frozen with fear.

"Get up!" hissed the spider.

She didn't move. The spider began walking toward her, moving so slowly that Willie wanted to scream to it to hurry up. But she made no sound, no motion, until she could feel the great creature stepping over her. Then, with a cry of triumph, she rolled over and thrust upward with her sword, burying it in the monster's hairy belly.

The spider's scream was terrible to hear. "Aaaaiiiieee! You got me, you wretched child! Aaarrrrgh. *Aaaarrrrrrghhh!*"

Staggering and groaning, it lurched into the forest and collapsed.

Scrambling to her feet, Willie looked at her sword in surprise. It was coated with green ichor. "I didn't know fighting a monster would be like . . . like *that*," she whispered, shivering.

"Hey, come on, boy—cut me down!" cried the bear.

"What? Oh! I almost forgot about you!"

"Great," muttered the bear. "You're supposed to be rescuing me, and instead you just forget me. Wonderful. I'm very amused."

"All right, all right, I'll get you loose," said Willie. After wiping her sword on some ferns to get rid of the spider goo, she cut the bear free from the web. It was about a foot taller than she was, roundish and furry. Its right ear was bent forward.

"Wow," it said, once she had it out of the web, "what a relief." It backed up to a tree and began to rub its shoulders against it.

"Glad to have been of service," said Willie. "Now, if you'll excuse me, I must return to my quest."

"Wait!" cried the bear when she turned to leave. "What kind of quest are you on?"

She smiled. "I'm going to kill the dragon."

The bear put its paws over its face. "You're crazy!" it said, peeking out from between them.

Willie shrugged. "Maybe. But I beat that spider, didn't I?"

The bear wrinkled its nose. After a moment it said, "You'd better let me come along. You saved my life. Maybe I can help you in return."

Willie looked at him. "I don't know. . . ."

"Never turn away a friend."

Before she could answer, they heard a roar not too far off. "That's him!" she cried. "Come on!"

She plunged through the underbrush, the bear following after her. But she was faster than the bear and soon had outdistanced it.

So she was the first to see how big the dragon really was.

8

Grizelda's Story

IN ANOTHER PART OF THE FOREST GRIZELDA AND Phrenella stood beside a bog, waiting for a squad of goons that was due to report on the dragon's doings.

"Well, boys, how's it going?" asked Grizelda when they came running into the clearing.

"Good!" cried the goon in the lead. "Good, good, very most good!"

"Yep yep yep!" said the second. "Today dragon burn down some trees . . ."

"And eat three cows . . ." interrupted another.

"And knock down a house when he burp!" cried a fourth.

Grizelda smiled and rubbed her hands. "Wonderful!" she cried. *"Wonderful!"*

But the smallest of the goons scratched its furry head and said, "We don't get one thing . . ."

"What's that?" asked Grizelda.

"We thought you make dragon to get king."

"I did!" she cried.

The goon crossed its eyes, a sign that it was thinking. "Then how come only peasants getting sad?" it asked at last.

Grizelda's own eyes grew wide, and her face twisted with rage. She flicked her hand to the right, and though she didn't touch the goon, it went flying across the clearing.

The other goons shrieked and ran into the forest.

"How dare you?" screamed Grizelda. "Of course the king will suffer! It just takes time for these troubles to reach him. That's all . . ." She paused. "Or is it?" she muttered. Letting out a long, low wail, she cried, "Phrenella, what have I done?"

Phrenella took Grizelda's arm and patted it. "Now, now, my dear," she said soothingly. "Wicked is wicked. The other girls are just thrilled at how evil your dragon is."

"But I didn't become a witch to be evil! I did it to get revenge on King Mildred!"

Phrenella looked at Grizelda curiously. "You

keep saying that. But you never told me what you want revenge *for*."

Grizelda closed her eyes for a moment. "Did you know my son had a birthmark?" she asked at last. "A dragon. It was on his shoulder. That's why I chose a dragon for my vengeance."

"What *are* you talking about?" asked Phrenella.

Grizelda made a gesture, and a giant mushroom sprouted beneath her hand. Settling onto it, she said, "Once, a long time ago, I was a mere peasant woman, just as normal as could be. I had a little house where I lived with my husband, who was very old, and my son, who was very young. Life was hard, but I was happy."

She paused to wipe away a tear, then lowered her hand when she remembered that witches can't cry.

"One day the king's men came riding up to the cottage and took my husband. They said there was a war, and he was needed to fight. I begged them not to take him away. 'We need him, too!' I told them. But they paid no heed to my cries of woe, and I watched in sorrow as they dragged my poor man away.

"After that, everything changed. I barely

51

slept, barely ate, mourning for my lost man, praying that he would survive the war. But when the war ended, he did not come back."

Phrenella sighed. "I love a sad ending," she said.

"Oh, but that was not the end at all," hissed Grizelda. "It was just the beginning of my sorrows. For though the war was over, it was not finished with me. Soldiers still wandered the countryside, wreaking havoc wherever they went. One day when I was working in the fields, they torched my cottage. When I trudged home at the end of the day, I found nothing but ashes. Now I had lost everything: house, husband, child. And that's when I went bad, Phrenella. I swore I would get revenge on the king if it was the last thing I ever did."

She paused, staring off into the distance. The goons, who had been hiding nearby to listen, began creeping back into the clearing.

"I searched for three years before I found a witch who was willing to make me her apprentice. I had to work for her for another three years—chop her wood, carry her water, scrub her floors—before she would even start to teach me what I wanted to know. But once she started, I studied like no pupil she had ever had, studied because of the revenge-fire burning in me. It made me want to learn more, faster, than anyone had ever learned before, so I could pay the king the debt of pain and sorrow that I owed him.

"For three years I studied day and night, night and day, barely sleeping, barely eating, just reading, learning, brewing, stewing, doing magic of all sorts. At the end of that time my teacher said, 'You have learned all that I can teach you,' and sent me back into the world.

"Now I knew the spell I wanted to cast. But it took another three years to gather all I needed to create a dragon that could work my will and wreak my revenge upon the king."

She closed her eyes and shook her head. "But was I wrong? Will I just make peasants suffer— peasants like myself, or at least the self I used to be?" She groaned. "Won't this pain ever reach the king?"

"I'm sure it will, my dear," said Phrenella, patting her arm again.

"That's the saddest story I ever heard," sniffed one of the goons, blowing its nose with a giant honk.

Grizelda's eyes widened as she realized that the creatures had slipped back into the clearing.

"What are you doing here?" she shrieked.

"Got one more thing to tell," said a goon nervously. "Important thing. Trouble is coming."

Grizelda's eyes widened. "What are you talking about?"

"Dragonslayers," it said. Then it covered its head with its arms, as if trying to shield itself from Grizelda's wrath.

It was a wise move. "Dragonslayers?" shrieked the witch, throwing a bolt of magic at the goon. *"Dragonslayers?"*

"Me didn't say it!" cried the goon. *"They* said it! Me heard them. Me sneaked and listened. They said king sent them to kill dragon. Me came to tell you."

"What a good goon you are," said Grizelda, calming down. She turned to the other goons. "Why can't the rest of you be as clever as Igbutton?" she shrieked, waving her hands and sending small bolts of power blasting in their direction.

Squealing and howling, the goons disappeared into the forest—all except the one who had brought the news about the Dragonslayers. He watched happily as Grizelda dug into one of the pockets of her robe and brought out a special treat, something she made herself just for rewarding goons who had been particularly useful. Smiling, she held the brownish-purple tidbit above the goon's head.

"Liver cookie!" cried Igbutton. "Oh gimme gimme gimme liver cookie! Thank you, thank you, thank you!"

Grizelda lowered the cookie. The goon snatched its treasure, then turned and ran into the forest.

Grizelda watched it leave. Then she turned to Phrenella and said, "We'd better split up. I want to find those Dragonslayers and put a stop to them. I've worked too hard for this dragon to let some 'hero' kill it before its flames sear the king's heart. Not that it will be easy to kill," she added with a chuckle, thinking of the magical protections she had placed on the dragon. "Not even possible for anyone who doesn't know its name."

Both witches cackled at the thought.

"If I find them, I'll fly them right to you," said Phrenella.

"And if *I* find them, there won't be enough left of them to fly anywhere," muttered Grizelda as she stalked into the darkness.

9

The Blessings of
the Forest

BRIAN, ELIZAR, AND THE FOX STOOD BESIDE A
fallen tree, looking around in confusion.

"I thought the roar came from that direction," said Brian, pointing to their right.

"I thought it came from over there," said Elizar, turning to the left.

"No," said the fox, pointing its nose straight ahead. "I'm sure it came from that way."

"Why don't we split up and do some scouting?" suggested Brian. "We can each look in the direction we thought the roar came from, then meet back here in fifteen minutes."

Elizar looked doubtful. "All right," he said

at last. "But don't try anything foolish. We're just *looking* for it right now. If you find the beast, come back here at once and call for me! We have to study it and make a plan."

"Of course!" said Brian. Pulling Dragonwhacker from its scabbard, he began walking in the direction he had chosen. He moved as silently as he could, not wanting the dragon to spot him before he spotted it.

When he had gone several hundred feet from the clearing, he suddenly stopped and looked around. "That's funny," he said. "For a second I thought I heard bells."

Looking down, he saw a fine mist creeping about his feet.

"What's going on here?" he muttered nervously.

Before he could decide whether to go forward or turn back, he began to feel enormously tired. Yawning, he raised his sword and turned in a slow circle, looking for an enemy. The mist, which was growing thicker, had risen so high that it was swirling around his knees.

Again, he heard the faint sound of bells. He tried to go on, but stumbled as sleep claimed him. He was unconscious by the time he hit the ground.

After a moment a slender form began to creep through the mist. Its skin was pale and its eyes were large. It was dressed in green and silver. Stopping a few feet from Brian, it stared at him with interest so intense it was almost like a longing.

Soon a similar being stepped from behind another of the great trees. This one, clearly female, joined the first, which was now kneeling beside Brian, studying him carefully. Setting one hand gently on the first being's shoulder, the newcomer whispered, "Tymbal—is he the one?"

It was not Tymbal who answered, but a third being. This one had stepped not from behind a tree, but right out of one. Stopping beside the others, he cocked his head and said, "He must be. The signs said this would be the time and place to find him."

The female shook her head. "Even so, we can't be sure, Vessan."

"We can never be *sure*, Florissa," said Tymbal. "We'll just have to trust him."

"Then shall we wake him?" asked Florissa.

Tymbal and Vessan hesitated, then nodded. All three bent above Brian. They began to hum a strange melody, its notes so gentle they

seemed to have been woven from the sound of wind moving through the leaves, the sound of water running over stones.

After a moment Brian stirred, causing the mist to swirl around him. Slowly he pushed himself to a sitting position. Blinking nervously, he said, "Who—who are you?"

"The spirits of the forest," said Tymbal. "We've come to seek your help—and to offer you ours."

Brian rubbed his hands over his face. "What do you mean?"

"We have a task for you," said Florissa urgently.

"An important one!" added Vessan.

"What is it?" asked Brian, groping for his sword.

"We want you to kill a dragon!"

"But that's why I'm here! I'm hunting for him right now!"

"I knew he was the one!" said Tymbal triumphantly.

Brian looked around. "At least, I *was* hunting for him. Then I fell asleep. Now, how did that happen?"

"*We* did it," said Florissa. "To make sure you were safe to talk to."

Brian shook his head. "What is this all about?" he asked, looking at the spirits through narrowed eyes.

"We are in terrible danger," said Tymbal. "The dragon is burning our trees. If he is not stopped, the forest will die."

The other two moaned. Florissa knelt in front of Brian and said, "If the forest dies, we die. . . ."

"Why?" asked Brian.

They answered together, speaking as if with one voice: "Because we are part of the forest."

"Well, stop worrying," said Brian, resting his hand on his sword. "I'm here to kill the beast."

"It is not that simple," said Tymbal. "The strength of one alone cannot do it."

"But the forest has powers to help," added a fourth spirit, who had somehow arrived without Brian noticing.

"What do you mean?" Brian asked.

"The old magic of the earth is strongest here in the forest," said Florissa. "If you reach out for it, it will give you strength."

Closing his eyes, Tymbal began to sing. His voice was high and clear.

"Old, strange and old
are the trees
in this great wood.
Roots run deep in the soil,
drawing strength
from the mother,
the earth;
silent trees, ancient trees
filled with the magic
of the earth—
in these trees
lie the blessings
of the forest."

Now the others joined him, singing of dewdrops that hung like diamonds along the edges of green leaves; of deep glades hedged in moonbeams; of water that laughed over polished stones to hidden pools, where you could find simple truths that would heal an aching heart.

"These are the blessings of the forest," said Tymbal.

Strangely moved by the song, Brian found himself brushing aside a tear. "It's lovely," he whispered. "But what does it have to do with me?"

"Don't you see?" asked Florissa. "You're part of the earth."

"Part of *everything*," said Tymbal.

"We all are," added Vessan. "But you mortals cut yourself off from the earth, and so lose its power and its strength."

"Alone, you can never conquer the dragon," said Tymbal impatiently. "But with the help of the forest, you can do it. The dragon is death, but the forest is life. The dragon wounds, but the forest heals. The dragon is fear, but the forest gives courage. You *must* understand."

The spirits surrounded Brian. Florissa, standing behind him, placed cool, slim hands over his eyes. "*Feel* the forest," she whispered. "Feel its roots going deep into the earth. Feel your own roots, tying you to the peace of the forest, to its strength."

"Reach out to the forest," said Tymbal. "It can help you. We have given—"

His words were cut off by a thunderous roar.

"The dragon!" cried the spirits. "He's nearby!"

In a moment they had vanished among the trees, so completely that Brian wondered if the entire thing had been a dream—until he heard Florissa's voice whisper to him from somewhere in the bushes, "*Remember!*"

"I will," he whispered back. "I promise."

Taking up his sword, he stood and began to move in the direction from which the roar had come. The dragon was closer than ever, he was sure of it.

A moment later he heard something large moving through the greenery. *Pheew!* he thought as a rank, sulphurous odor assaulted his nostrils. *I hope it doesn't look as bad as it smells!*

He moved past another tree and stopped in horror. The dragon was less than fifty feet ahead of him. And it didn't look as bad as it smelled.

It looked worse.

10

Joining Forces

Willie stared at the dragon in astonishment. Covered with metallic-looking bronze scales, it had a head that was easily twice as long as that of the largest horse. Broad at the top, it tapered to a pointed snout that curved down like a bird's beak. A handspan back from the tip of the snout flared a pair of nostrils from which curled plumes of blue smoke. The nostrils, each the size of a man's fist, widened and dilated as the dragon breathed.

The mouth extended three quarters of the way along the head. Glistening fangs curved up from the lower jaw. Above each end of the mouth slanted an enormous yellow-green eye, slit by a vertical black pupil. Farther back along the head flared a pair of spiky, spiny ears.

Seven or eight feet farther back still, just above the front legs, sprouted a pair of batlike wings. Ten feet beyond them were the hind legs. A row of spines, something like the fin on the back of a fish, only higher and sharper, ran from the crown of the head to the tip of the lashing tail. The tail itself was curling, twisting and coiling so fast that there was no way Willie could guess its actual length.

The great head moved slowly back and forth, as if the beast was seeking something. All plans of slaying the monster slipped from Willie's mind as she froze, wondering if it had somehow sensed her presence.

So intent was she on staying silent that she didn't notice someone slipping up behind her until she heard a branch snap. Barely avoiding a gasp that might have betrayed her to the dragon, she swung to her right.

Brian was standing nearby. He looked as surprised as she felt—though whether he recognized her, or was simply surprised to find anyone else stalking the dragon, she could not tell. Suddenly she realized that Brian's gaze had shifted from her to the dragon. The look of horror in his eyes made her turn back herself. Again she stifled a gasp.

The dragon was looking their way.

Now she dared not even breathe, for fear of attracting its attention. But though the beast continued to stare in their direction, the thickness of the forest worked in their favor, hiding them from its eyes. After a seemingly endless moment, it turned and continued on its way.

Willie relaxed and let out a sigh.

"Who are you?" hissed Brian. "What are you doing here?"

Willie was about to ask how he dared speak to her like that when she remembered her disguise. She knew that the most effective part of the charade was not her clothing, but the fact that no one would ever expect to find the Princess Wilhelmina wandering the forest dressed as a boy. Lowering her voice, she said, "My name is . . . Bill. I was looking for the dragon."

Before Brian could ask why, they heard a rustling in the bushes. Still edgy with the memory of the dragon, they both jumped.

"Did you find it?" asked Elizar, thrashing his way through the brush with the fox close behind him.

Before Brian could answer, the bear came rushing in from the other direction.

"I saw the dragon!" it squeaked. It stopped, lowered its voice, tried again. "I saw the dragon. It's even bigger than before!"

That was the last anyone said for a moment, as they all stood and stared at one another.

"Who's this?" asked Elizar at last, pointing to Willie.

"He says his name is Bill," said Brian.

"Hello, Bill," said Elizar gently. "You'd better go home now. There's a dragon loose, and—"

"I know all about the dragon!" snapped Willie.

Elizar looked startled. "Then what are you doing here?"

"He . . . took something that belongs to me," said Willie. "I want it back." To herself she thought: *What he took was my freedom, and I don't intend to give it up by marrying you!*

"Well, you can just run along," said Brian cheerfully. "We're on the job now."

Willie's eyes flashed. "As long as that dragon's loose, *I'm* hunting for him."

"Then why not come with us?" asked Elizar. "After all, the more help the better!"

Willie looked at him in surprise. "Aren't you out for a reward?" she asked.

Elizar made one of his clanking shrugs. "A

reward would be nice. I'm a lot more interested in getting rid of this dragon for the king."

This answer was even more surprising to Willie than the offer to let her accompany them. But before she could think about it, Brian narrowed his eyes and asked, "How do *you* know about the reward?"

Willie tried desperately to come up with some answer that would not give away her disguise, but nothing she thought of seemed very convincing. Just as her silence was becoming suspicious, she was saved by the fox.

"Good heavens!" it exclaimed. "Word of King Mildred's promise is all over the forest. Everyone is wondering whether he'll keep his word if someone actually does manage to slay the dragon." It paused, then added, "Well, everyone figures he'll be glad to give up his daughter's hand in marriage. What they're really wondering is whether he'll give up half the kingdom as well."

Willie started to squawk in indignation, but caught herself and turned the sound into a cough.

"I don't know," said Brian uneasily. "This is supposed to be *our* job."

"And we're going to need all the help we can

get," said Elizar. "I don't care *how* it gets done, as long as done it gets. Bill, I think the smartest thing would be for you to come with us."

For a moment Willie thought about breaking from the group and running into the forest. But Elizar's words had confused and surprised her. Between the fact that she wanted to learn more about the old man, and the fact that it was nice to have a little company, she decided she would stay with the group until nightfall, and then slip away when she had the chance. After all, she did still plan to kill the dragon herself—though now that she had seen the thing, she realized it was a bigger problem than she had expected.

With a nod to Elizar she said, "I guess you're right."

The bear sighed with relief. "Good. Maybe together we can live through this."

Brian sighed, too. He knew he had to accept Bill's decision to join them. But he so desperately wanted to be the one to kill the dragon himself that it hurt to add anyone else to the expedition. Trying to hide his disappointment, he turned to Elizar and said, "It might be best at that. Now that I've seen the thing, I don't know *how* we're going to kill it."

"You saw it?" asked Elizar in surprise.

Brian nodded. "It's much bigger than that peasant woman said."

Elizar groaned. Willie nearly suggested that he return to the castle himself, but managed to bite her lip instead.

"Better tell me about him," said the old man.

Brian and Willie both launched into descriptions of the monster. Their words tumbled over each other as they talked of its great size and terrible fierceness.

"We need to make a battle plan," said Elizar when they were done. He looked around. "It's getting late. Why don't we find a place to make camp for the night? If we rest for a bit, maybe we'll be able to think more clearly."

Finding a place to rest turned out to be more difficult than they expected. Two hours later they were still trudging wearily through the forest.

"My feet are killing me," moaned the bear, picking up a paw and shaking it. "Can't we stop soon?"

"Look!" said Willie. "A little way past that big tree. See? There's a clearing with a cottage at the far side. Maybe we can find supper and a place to rest there."

"Good idea," said Elizar, lifting his visor to squint into the green gloom that surrounded them.

However, as they drew closer to the clearing, the fox's bushy tail began twitching nervously. "This isn't such a good idea after all," the creature muttered.

"Why not?" asked Brian.

Glancing from side to side, as if it expected to find a spy under any fern, the fox whispered, "That cottage belongs to *Grizelda!*"

11

Royal Pain

IN ANOTHER PART OF THE FOREST A NEW GROUP OF questers trudged wearily into a clearing. The group was led by King Mildred, who had dragged his knights into the forest with him to seek not the dragon, but Willie. Queen Hortense was with them, too, for she had insisted that she would not be left behind while her daughter was in danger. Even the page boys had been forced to come along. (The maids-in-waiting, of course, had been expected to stay home.)

"Don't you think we've looked long enough, Your Majesty?" moaned Sir Pentamon.

"Nonsense," snapped the king, who had dark circles under his eyes. "We won't stop until we find her!"

The knights all groaned.

"Can we at least take a rest?" asked Sir Wexler. It turned out that his armor really was leaking, and he had water in his boots.

"I suppose so," growled the king. "But not for long!"

Wearily the knights and page boys collapsed to the ground.

"Come and sit over here, my dear," said the queen, leading the king to a mossy spot in the clearing.

"I don't know why he wants her back so badly," whispered Sir Filibuster, who was quite disgruntled about the fact that he had been forced to leave the castle and wander around in the forest. "Things at court haven't been this calm for years!"

Sir Pentamon nodded in agreement. "I haven't found a frog in my armor since she left."

"It's fish I'm worried about," said Sir Wexler, pulling off his boot and dumping out the water.

Across the clearing King Mildred was sitting on a tree stump while the queen rubbed his neck. His feet were surrounded by new growth that had sprouted from the base of the stump.

"You must try to relax, my dear," said the queen.

"I can't!" he cried. "I keep going over things

in my mind, trying to figure out what went wrong." He closed his eyes. After a moment he whispered, "I should have been more understanding, I can see that now. Oh, Hortense, I had such high hopes when Wilhelmina was born. I still remember every detail of that day. She was so tiny, so . . . perfect. And now she's gone!"

"We'll find her," said the queen firmly.

"I wish I could be sure of that," said the king. "Even if we do, I don't know if it will be enough. What I really want back is the time. I want her to be a baby again, so I can protect her, and so she'll believe in me."

He slipped his hand over the queen's. "Where *does* the time go?" he whispered. "It flowed by so fast, and now I have no more idea where it has gone than I do where Wilhelmina is."

"What will you do if we find her?" asked the queen gently. "Things won't be any different, you know. You're both very stubborn—and you both want different things."

"Right now I just want her to be safe," said the king. "I wish she could understand how much I love her, how much I miss her."

"I miss her, too," said the queen. "I even miss her crazy dreams." Settling beside the king, she laid her head on his knees and whispered, "Why is it we never tell the people we love the things they need to hear? We were so busy trying to get her to be the kind of daughter *we* wanted, we never listened to her telling us what kind of person *she* wanted to be." She sighed. "People are so strange. Why are the things we love the things we're most likely to attack?"

"The thing we need to attack right now is that dragon," said the king. "We *must* find it before she does." Staggering to his feet, he cried, "Come on, men—let's go."

Groaning, the knights and the page boys fell into line as the king once more led the way into the forest.

In another part of the forest Grizelda was pacing back and forth in her cottage, muttering to herself about the dragon and whether it would actually work her revenge on the king. She stopped to stir the green brew bubbling over her fire—she was cooking up a special spell that she hoped would help her locate the Dragonslayers—then turned to start pacing again.

Her fretting was interrupted by Igbutton

scrambling through her window. "Someone's coming!" hissed the goon. *"Someone's coming!"*

"Who?" asked Grizelda.

"Don't know, don't know. But there are lots of them. Igbutton counted!" It held up its fingers to show her as it ticked off the list: "One, two, lots!" it said proudly.

"All right," she said impatiently. "That's fine. Now be off!"

"Did good?" asked the little goon. "Did good?"

"You did *fine!*" shrieked Grizelda. "Now go!"

"Cookie?" it pleaded.

Grizelda sighed and dug one of the liver cookies out of her robe. "Here," she said, tossing it to the goon. "Now be gone!"

Clutching the cookie, squealing with fear, Igbutton scurried back over the windowsill.

Grizelda stood in thought for a moment, then cast a spell over her house to make it appear as if it were empty. That way she could study the newcomers in safety. Crossing to her window, she waited for the Dragonslayers to arrive.

12

Grizelda's Curse

"MY FEET DON'T HURT ANYMORE!" SAID THE BEAR, glancing uneasily toward Grizelda's cottage. "Honest!"

"Don't be silly," said Brian. "This is great! Maybe we can trick her into telling us something about the dragon."

They had nearly reached the edge of the clearing. Standing on its hind legs, the bear began to do a little dance. "Look!" it cried. "It's a miracle! My feet really do feel better."

"Well, mine don't," said Elizar. "In fact, I think I've got a stone in my boot. Wait a minute, while I get it out."

He plunked himself down on a stump that stood just inside the clearing. To his astonish-

ment—and everyone else's, for that matter—
the stump let out a loud yowl.

With a clatter of armor, Elizar leapt to his
feet. "What was that?" he cried.

"It must have come from the cottage," said the
fox. "I'm sure Grizelda keeps a cat or so around."

Since this seemed far more sensible than
thinking that the yowl had actually come from
the stump, the others agreed that the fox must
be right.

Elizar sat down again.

Yowwwwlll!

Elizar fell off the stump. "Cottage my foot!"
he yelped. "That came from underneath me!"

"That's crazy!" protested Willie.

Brian snorted. "We're lost in a forest where
witches *make* dragons, and you think a stump
can't yowl?"

"Well, it doesn't make any sense," muttered Willie.

"Maybe it's not really a stump," said Brian,
helping Elizar to his feet.

"You mean it might be someone under a
spell?" asked the fox.

"I like that idea!" cried the bear. "Let's try
to break it!"

The fox made a little sniff of disdain. "Now,

how would we do that? We don't know what kind of a spell it is."

"Probably it needs to be kissed," said Willie. "Why don't you give it a try, Brian?"

Brian rolled his eyes. "Very funny, Bill."

"I think Bill is serious," said Elizar, struggling with the kneejoint of his armor, which had locked in place when he fell.

"Then let him kiss it!" snapped Brian.

"Wouldn't do any good," said Willie cheerfully. "I'm just a peasant boy. You're the closest thing we have to a handsome prince."

Brian scowled, but the fox said, "Why not give it a try, Master? It couldn't hurt—and it might help."

Brian hesitated. On the one hand, he might look like a real idiot. On the other hand, if the stump really was under an enchantment, breaking the spell would be a very heroic thing to do. Finally he walked to the stump. After staring at it for a moment, he knelt and moved his face toward it. Then he shook his head and backed away.

"Just do it!" cried Willie, barely able to contain her laughter.

Making a face, Brian bent forward and pressed his lips to the thick, rough bark.

Nothing happened.

"Ptoooie!" he said, rubbing his mouth with his sleeve.

Willie started to laugh. Brian glared at the disguised princess and said, "At least I was willing to try, Bill."

"Maybe you have to keep trying until you find the part that used to be its lips!" replied Willie merrily. After a moment she added, "I wonder what part you kissed that time?"

Brian blinked, then rubbed his mouth again.

"Well, the whole thing has me stumped," said Elizar. "And I still have to get rid of this stone."

Leaning against a tree, he pulled off his boot. When he turned it over, out rolled a large, sharp pebble.

"No wonder it hurt," said Elizar, rubbing his bony foot. "Wait for me while I go rinse this bruise in that stream we passed a way back."

Picking up his boot, he hobbled into the forest.

The others stood at the edge of the clearing, glancing nervously at Grizelda's cottage. It seemed innocent enough—a low, thatch-roofed dwelling nestled at the base of an enormous tree. But the bear's fear was catching, and they were all just as glad that Elizar's foot had given them an excuse to put off approaching the cottage.

After a moment Willie and the bear drifted to one side of the clearing, Brian and the fox to the other. As they settled down to wait for Elizar, the fox turned to Brian and said, "You seem anxious to slay the dragon yourself, Master."

Though she could not be seen by the questers, Grizelda was leaning out her window to watch them.

"Too far away," she muttered after a moment. "I can't hear them."

Waving her hands, she worked a minor magic to bring her enemies' words more clearly to her ears.

It took effect just in time for her to hear the fox's remark about Brian wanting to slay the dragon.

"So *he's* the king's Dragonslayer," she muttered. "He's awfully young for it. King Mildred must be getting pretty desperate. Well, I'm not ready to have this game end yet. I'd best put a stop to that one's plans right now."

She rolled up her sleeves, then waved her skinny arms and chanted:

THE DRAGONSLAYERS

"Spirits of the dark and gloom
Cast a spell of pain and doom:
Stay his hand when dragon nears
And let his quest bring pain and tears!"

"There," she whispered when she was done. "That should take care of *him*. Now he'll never kill the dragon!"

13

Grizelda's Cure

BRIAN SHOOK HIS HEAD AS A SHIVER RAN DOWN HIS spine.

"Are you all right?" yipped the fox.

"I think so," he replied, looking a little dazed. "I just had a chill was all. What were you asking me?"

"About slaying the dragon," said the fox, looking at him carefully.

"Right, the dragon." Brian glanced around. Seeing that the peasant boy and the bear were out of earshot, he whispered, "Let me show you something—something I've never shown anyone else." Reaching up with his left hand, he pulled his collar down to bare his right shoulder.

"A dragon!" whispered the fox in astonishment.

Brian nodded. "It's my birthmark. I've always felt my fate must be connected to a dragon somehow. When news of this one reached the court, I was sure I was destined to kill it."

Grizelda almost fell out of her window when she heard Brian's words about the dragon birthmark.

"My son!" she whispered to herself. "My son is alive! He's *alive!*"

Then she caught her breath in horror as she realized what she had just done.

"My son," she moaned. "I've cursed my own son!"

Elizar reentered the clearing. He had his boot back on his foot and a battered tin cup in his right hand. "Aaah," he said, sipping from the cup. "That is delicious!"

He was so busy concentrating on the water that he didn't notice the stone in his path until he tripped over it. Stumbling, he spilled the clear springwater all over the stump.

With a flash and a roar the stump vanished in a puff of green smoke. In its place sat a large yellow cat which stretched hugely, then rubbed against Elizar's leg. "Thank you!" it purred. "I thought I would never get out of that stump!"

"Look!" cried Elizar in astonishment. "I rescued someone!"

"What's going on?" asked the cat, glancing around. "A party? Grizelda *never* has this many visitors."

"Grizelda doesn't seem to be around," said Elizar through his visor, which had fallen over his face when he tripped.

"Don't be too sure," said the cat. "A couple of months ago I thought she was miles away and stole some cream. Turned out she was right beside me, using a spell to hide herself. That's when she transformed me into a tree stump."

The bear growled and looked over its shoulder nervously.

"How cruel!" said Willie.

"I agree," said the cat, stretching again. "So tell me: *Why* are you all here?"

"To slay the dragon!" said Brian.

"Don't say that!" hissed the cat. "Around here even the corn has ears! Why, one day—"

Before it could finish, Grizelda came swooping into the clearing on her broomstick. The fox and the bear dove for cover as she landed. Willie and Brian reached for their swords. Elizar jumped back, causing his visor—which he had just managed to get in place—to flop down again.

"Save me!" cried the cat, running to the old knight. "Save me!"

"Well, this is quite a gathering," sneered Grizelda. "What do you want here?"

"Nothing," said Elizar, struggling with his visor. "I . . ."

He stopped, as if the words had lodged in his throat. Grizelda, too, seemed struck by something strange. She stared at him for a moment, then turned her attention to the cat.

"I see you've been rescued, Master Puss. Shall I work up a new spell for you?"

"No!" shouted Elizar.

"So, Master Puss has a protector!" cackled Grizelda. "Well, if he wants you, cat, he can have you. You're worthless to me. You're all worthless. So you'd better leave my home now—while you still can!"

For a moment no one moved. Brian, Willie, and the animals stared at Grizelda with a combination of fascination and fear that seemed to have them frozen in their tracks. Finally Elizar said, "She's right. We don't belong here. Come on, we'll rest elsewhere."

With Elizar leading the way, they began to

leave the clearing. Brian was last to go, and he kept looking back over his shoulder, as if reluctant to leave for some reason.

Grizelda gestured to him.

"You," she said. "Come here."

He looked about uncertainly. Grizelda beckoned again. "Yes, boy," she hissed. "I mean you."

Brow knit, moving slowly, Brian approached the witch. She reached out and grabbed him by the chin. Her fingers felt like the claws of a small dragon. Closing one eye, she examined him carefully, turning his face from side to side. Finally she sighed and let him go.

"I have something for you," she said. She rummaged in her cape for a moment, finally pulling from some hidden pocket a small green bottle. She held it out to him. "Take this. You may need it."

Brian looked at her curiously. "What is it?"

"A healing potion. It will cure almost any wound. Pour it on the wound, then cover it with your hand. You must hold your hand in place until the healing is complete! If you don't, the potion won't work."

"Why are you giving this to me?" asked Brian, curiosity replaced by suspicion.

"Do you want it or not?" she snapped.

"Yes, but—"

"Then take it! Take it, and go!"

Still he hesitated, confused.

"Leave!" she shrieked.

He raced from the clearing, stumbling as he looked back. Grizelda watched until he was lost from her sight. Then she returned to her cottage. Laying her head on a table covered with magical items, wishing that she could weep, she moaned, "My son, my *son* . . ."

14

Heartless

Two hours later the Dragonslayers had gathered about a small campfire. The forest was dark now, and the wind moving through the trees made strange noises that kept them from relaxing.

They were eating a vegetable stew that Elizar had concocted from roots he dug up as they traveled. While they ate, the cat told them what it had seen the night Grizelda made the dragon.

"It's amazing," muttered Elizar, mopping up a bit of gravy with one of the biscuits (which he had also made).

"That's not all," said the cat. "According to what I heard Grizelda say, the dragon can't be killed in any of the usual ways."

"Are you serious?" asked Willie.

"Absolutely," said the cat, licking a paw and wiping it over one ear. "She placed a lot of protection spells on it. Then she took out its heart. Magicked it out."

"Took out its heart?" asked Brian, blinking in confusion. "I don't understand."

"I do," said the fox. "Usually you kill a dragon by putting a sword through its heart. But if it doesn't have a heart . . ."

Elizar put down his plate. "Isn't there *any* way to kill this monster?" he asked, pulling at his beard.

The fire snapped, sending sparks spiraling into the night sky. The cat thought for a second. "I did hear Grizelda tell her friend Phrenella that the dragon would be vulnerable to someone who knew its name."

"Did she say what its name was?" asked Willie eagerly.

The cat shook its head. "Phrenella asked her. But she said that a side effect of casting the spell was that she could never reveal the name herself."

"Well, I wouldn't worry about it too much," said Brian, who was sitting beside the fire sharpening Dragonwhacker. "I still think some cold steel will do the job."

Peeking out from under its tail, which it had wrapped over its nose, the fox said, "Maybe, maybe not. You never can tell with these witchy critters."

Brian shivered, but didn't answer. After a moment he got up and walked to the edge of the clearing, where he stood staring into the darkness. He was still baffled by his encounter with Grizelda, and he was trying to figure out what it meant.

After a few minutes Willie went to stand next to Brian. The moon was on his face. Making sure that she herself stayed in darkness, she studied him.

"You seem eager to slay the dragon yourself, Brian," she said at last. "I thought it was supposed to be Elizar's job."

"It is," he answered, not turning to look at her. "But who knows? I might get a chance." After a pause, he added, "Boy, would I love that!"

"Why?"

He shrugged. "I've always had big dreams. And I want to prove something to the other page boys. You're just a peasant, so you can't imagine what it's like at court, Bill. The others are always laughing at me for trying too hard. I want to prove what I can do."

"And that's it?" asked Willie.

Brian was silent for a moment. The forest whispered around them, sounds of wind, of night animals, of singing insects. Finally he said, "No. I want to prove something to myself, too. Did you ever lie awake at night, wondering who you are, why you're here?"

"A lot," said Willie.

Brian shrugged. "I thought slaying a dragon might give me some answers."

Willie tried to hide her surprise. There was more to Brian than she had realized. She waited a moment, then asked, "What about the reward? Is that part of it?"

Brian laughed. "Half the kingdom? Sure, who wouldn't want that?"

"And the king's daughter?" she asked, feeling bold.

Brian snorted. "That nut? You've got to be kidding!"

"How can you talk that way about a princess?" cried Willie.

"You never met her, Bill. She wants to be a knight, of all things. She's always getting in trouble around the castle; thinks she can do things just like a boy. I don't know why her father doesn't give her a good spanking."

Willie made a little choking sound as she tried to keep herself from screaming. She held her breath for a moment, then said, "Well, at least she wants to do something."

"That's true," Brian admitted. He thought for a second, then added, "You know, she might be almost human, if she weren't a princess."

Willie's eyes blazed. It was all she could do to keep from sweeping off her hat, letting down her hair, and demanding, "What's wrong with princesses?" After a struggle she swallowed hard and asked the question quietly, trying to sound surprised, instead of furious.

Brian shrugged. "Nothing that a little taste of the real world wouldn't cure, I guess. But you'd never catch one of the royal family out here trying to kill a dragon. They're too interested in their own skins."

Willie was wondering whether it would be worth ruining her disguise to punch him in the nose when the bear interrupted them with an enormous yawn. "Boy, am I tired," it said. "Let's get to sleep. We've got a big day ahead of us."

"Good idea," purred the cat, which had already curled up beside the fire.

"I agree," said Elizar. "If we get a good rest now, we can get up with the sun and look for fewmets."

"Fewmets?" asked the yawning bear.

"He means dragon droppings," explained Willie, turning away from Brian.

"Eeeeuw!" cried the bear. "That's disgusting!"

"Elizar's right," said Brian. "If we're going to be ready tomorrow, we'd better sleep now. Good night, everyone."

The others said their good-nights and lay down to sleep. But sleep was not quick in coming. Each lay staring into the darkness, thinking about the dragon, wondering what it would mean when they finally found it.

Still, one by one, they drifted into a restless slumber—all except Willie, who waited until everyone's breathing seemed steady and settled. Then she rolled over. Closing her hand over the bear's snout, she whispered in its ear, "Wake up."

It tried to snort, but Willie's hand held the sound in. "Shhh!" she hissed. "Don't say a thing."

She waited for the bear to stop struggling, then took her hand from its snout. "Come on! We have to get going."

When the bear started to ask why, she tapped it sharply on the nose and shook her head. "I have to kill the dragon myself," she whispered. "I'll explain later."

Shaking its head, the bear followed her into the forest.

The others got another hour of sleep before the dragon arrived.

15

Enter the Dragon

AN ENORMOUS ROAR SHATTERED THE SILENCE OF the night.

"Did you hear that?" cried Brian, leaping to his feet.

The fire had died to coals, giving him only the faintest light as he scrambled for his sword.

"It sounded terribly close," said Elizar, sitting up more slowly.

"Where's Bill?" asked the fox.

"Looks like the coward disappeared," said Brian. "I didn't think . . ."

Before he could finish, the dragon roared again.

"It's closer," hissed the cat. "It's coming this way!"

A moment later a column of flame shot straight into the air, casting a garish mix of harsh light and deep shadow across the little band as it scrambled to get ready to face the monster's arrival.

Brian helped Elizar buckle his armor. When they were done, the old knight drew his sword and said, "This could be it, Brian. You and the others get back that way."

"What do you mean?" cried Brian.

"I want you out of harm's way. If I fall, then it will be your job to try next."

"But—"

"Brian, the king laid this task on me. I may not prevail, but it is my duty, and I must—"

He was interrupted by another roar from the dragon. It was very close now.

"Get back!" ordered Elizar with a strength Brian had never before heard in his voice. And because the old man was right—because he was the knight and Brian the squire, Brian had no choice but to obey.

"This way," he called to the fox and the cat, who were obviously far happier to leave the battle to Elizar than he was. "We'll watch from here."

It was possible that the dragon was merely passing by. But each of them had a sense that this time he was not just coming in their direction, but coming *for* them, to get them. The cat was tense and alert, only the tip of its tail twitching, twitching. The fox stood beside Brian, saying nothing but pressed close to his leg. Brian held Dragonwhacker firmly, ready to rush in should Elizar need his help.

Elizar himself stood in the center of the clearing, straight and tall, sword drawn, facing the darkness from which the roar was coming.

Suddenly the dragon burst through the trees. Despite himself, Brian screamed.

"Heee-yah!" cried Elizar. Swinging his sword, he went clanking toward the dragon as fast as he could while wearing his heavy armor.

The dragon lashed out with its right foreleg, swooping the old knight into the air and sending him smashing against a tree. With a clatter of armor, he slid to the ground.

"Elizar!" cried Brian.

The old man lay silent and unmoving.

Breaking away from the animals, Brian rushed toward the fallen knight. The dragon roared—a terrible sound that shook the night—and swung its head toward Brian. As it did, the fox raced through the undergrowth. Bursting into the far side of the clearing, it leapt upon the dragon's tail.

The monster twisted angrily and shot a blast of flame into the darkness. The fox squealed and jumped aside, barely managing to avoid having its tail turned into a torch.

Knowing that the dragon would have to wait before it could manage another belch of fire, the cat hissed, drawing the dragon's attention from the fox. With a roar the beast turned toward the cat, which was scrambling up a tree.

While the animals distracted the dragon, Brian knelt at Elizar's side.

"It's too late to help me," moaned the old knight. "Go kill the dragon."

Brian glanced up at the dragon. Terrifying as it was, he longed to stand against it, to raise his sword in battle. Here at last was his chance to prove what he could do. But if he did, Elizar would surely die. He had to use Grizelda's potion first. If the cat and the fox could keep the dragon distracted long enough, they might all escape.

"I have something that can help," he said, unbuckling the old man's chest plate. He gasped when he saw the terrible wound that gaped beneath the armor. After fumbling in his pouch, he drew forth the little bottle.

"Brian," wheezed Elizar. "The dragon . . ."

"I'll take my chances!" said Brian as the

dragon swatted the fox away from its tail. With a yowl the cat leapt through the air and landed on the dragon's neck. The beast flipped its head, sending the cat sailing into the branches of a pine tree. It continued to hiss and spit, but the dragon ignored it now. Turning, it began to advance on Brian and Elizar.

"Brian!" shouted Elizar. "Leave me! You have to fight him."

"I can't!" cried Brian desperately as he struggled to pull the cork from the potion bottle. Finally he used his teeth to get it loose. "There!" he gasped as he poured the glowing green liquid onto Elizar's wound. "Now I have to hold you until this works! Then we'll get out of here together and figure out some way to—"

His words were cut off by another roar as the dragon began to close in for the kill.

The fox attacked it from behind, trying to distract it again. The cat went racing under its belly. But the monster's attention was focused on Brian and Elizar, and it would not be turned away.

"Leave me," gasped Elizar.

"Never!" whispered Brian.

Holding his hand over Elizar's wound, he stared straight ahead, into the face of death.

16

The Secret Name

THE DRAGON OPENED ITS MOUTH. BRIAN WASN'T sure whether it had had time to prepare another blast of flame or was simply planning to bite off his head.

Before the beast could do either, it was distracted by a new voice.

"Yeee-hah!" cried Willie. She came swinging into the clearing on a vine, waving her sword above her head. A fierce joy lit her face. "Not so fast, dragon," she said, dropping to the ground. "There's one more sword to face today."

The dragon turned, roaring ferociously.

Sword poised, Willie crouched for battle.

To her astonishment, the dragon spoke.

"Fool!" it roared in a voice that sounded like rocks grinding together.

Willie gasped and took a step back. Then she seemed to recover. Raising her sword, she cried, "Have at thee, beast!"

"Twice a fool to face my power," hissed the monster. Then it smiled, which somehow made it twice as terrifying. "Dragons are not taken so easily. Dragons do not die so fast."

Willie stood as if frozen, staring into the beast's great eyes.

Brian, who was kneeling with Elizar's head in his lap, could sense the dragon's voice weaving a spell, capturing Bill with its magic. He watched in horror as the peasant boy's sword began to droop.

"Yes!" roared the dragon. "Look at me, fool, and learn what fear really is. Feel it! Feel the fear that freezes bones. Look into my eyes and see the hatred that fueled my creation. Then let your blood run cold with *fear!*"

As Brian watched, the peasant boy began to sway. Soon he looked as if he were about to fall over.

The dragon chuckled, causing smoke to curl from its nose.

Suddenly Brian heard the sound of bells from somewhere nearby.

"Remember!" whispered a familiar voice. *"Remember."*

He closed his eyes. The power of the forest! But what good could it do him now?

No point in asking. He simply had to find it, touch it. Closing his eyes, he tried to open himself to the forest. All at once he felt its power moving within him—felt it, and knew the answer.

"Bill!" he cried. "Listen to me! The dragon feeds on fear. Fear is his weapon, the source of his strength. You have to *let go* of your fear!"

"Silence, fool!" roared the dragon, whipping around to glare at Brian.

Brian flinched at the sight of those great yellow eyes. He could feel the fear starting to move through him again. He wanted to drop Elizar and run to save his own life. He fought to keep himself connected to the forest, to the earth. Though he trembled, he held his hand over Elizar's wound, praying that it would heal soon.

The dragon started toward him.

At that moment the bear ran into the clearing. "Bill!" it cried. "Where did you . . ." Its voice tailed off as it saw the dragon. "Uh-oh," it whispered. It began backing away from the great beast. On the third step it bumped into Willie.

*   *   *

Willie had been watching the dragon move toward Brian and thinking in a distracted way that the page boy was very brave to sit there, so solid and unmoving. But when the bear bumped into her it broke her out of her stupor.

What am I doing? she thought, shaking her head. She stared at her sword as if seeing it for the first time. Suddenly she understood Brian's words—even as Brian himself was about to die.

"No!" she cried, raising the sword. "Not Brian! No! No!"

Something strange and powerful began to flow through her. And as her fear disappeared she suddenly knew the dragon's name. Swinging the sword above her head, she cried, "Turn and look at me, *Fear.* That is your name, isn't it? *Fear?*"

Slowly the dragon turned away from Brian, toward Willie.

"Wretched child!" it hissed. "Who told you my name?"

"No one," said Willie, crouching and tightening her grip on her sword. "No one told me. But I have named you, and so I have tamed you, and now it is time for you to die!"

The dragon began to crawl toward her. "Fear me," it hissed.

"I do not," said Willie.

"Fear me," it repeated, moving even closer. The great head was within striking distance, the enormous eyes glaring at her. But the voice was softer, almost pleading.

"I do not," repeated Willie firmly.

The dragon took a deep breath. It began to tremble. "Fear me," it said, its voice no more than a whisper. "Fear . . ."

With a sigh, it fell to its side, and spoke no more.

Willie stood in triumph, staring at the dragon. Brian bit his lip, looking at a dream dissolved.

The moment was shattered by a cry from Elizar. "Brian! It hurts! It *hurts!*"

The old man's body arched wildly, then relaxed. Taking a deep breath, he looked up at Brian and whispered, "You saved me."

"I'm glad," said Brian. "But Bill has killed the dragon."

Elizar closed his eyes. "It was the task that counted, Brian, not the hand that did it."

"I know," whispered Brian. "I know. But still . . ."

His words hung in the air for a moment. Before he could think of how to say what he was feeling, what was inside him, a trumpet sounded through the forest. A moment later King Mildred and Queen Hortense came rushing into the clearing, followed by the knights and the pages, who were moving rather more slowly.

All stopped in astonishment when they saw the dragon's body. Approaching it cautiously, the king prodded at the creature with his foot. It twitched, causing the knights to scream and jump backward. But other than that twitch, the dragon lay still, even when the king kicked it again.

"The beast is dead!" he cried, astonishment and relief mingled in his voice. "Who killed it?"

Willie bowed her head in what looked like modesty, in order to hide her face from her father.

17

The Rest of the Secrets

King Mildred walked to the peasant boy. "Are you the hero who has done this great deed?" he asked in surprise.

Willie was silent. The answer came from Brian, who still knelt at the edge of the clearing with Elizar's head on his knees.

"Yes, it was him, Your Highness. And a brave deed it was, too!"

Willie threw him a grateful look.

"Then I shall knight the lad!" said the king, rather pompously.

Brian hesitated, then said, "I believe there was more to it than that, Sire. . . ."

The king glanced at him sharply. "What do you mean?" he asked, sounding more nervous than pompous this time.

"Half the kingdom?" said Elizar helpfully.

The king began to sputter. "Well . . . I mean . . . why . . . *Harrumph!*"

"Those *were* your words, my dear," said the queen, putting her hand on his arm.

The king chewed his lip and muttered into his beard, but finally said, "Oh, all right. Half the kingdom is yours, lad."

"Thank you, my liege," said Willie, still looking down. "But I must tell you that I have heard that there was still more."

"What?" cried the king, outraged.

"Did you not promise your daughter's hand to whoever killed the dragon?"

The king's eyes flashed dangerously. "Don't be ridiculous! If you were a knight, of course. But you're a mere bumpkin. You have half my kingdom. Be reasonable."

"Was it not your promise?" asked Willie, her voice firm.

Brian looked on in astonishment, hardly able to believe that this peasant boy could stand up to the king. Elizar pulled himself to a sitting position to better watch the show.

As for the king, he began to sputter. "Yes, it was," he said, sounding desperate. "But if my daughter—"

"A promise is a promise—especially when made by a king," said Willie.

"But really . . . ," said King Mildred. "You don't know her. She'll . . ." He stopped, uncertain of what to say. Finally he looked to the queen for help.

He didn't find much. "I hate to say it," said the queen, "but the lad is right. At least he'll be able to support her," she added rather sharply, "since he owns half the kingdom!"

The king sighed. "All right—my daughter's hand is yours!"

"Then my life is my own!" cried Willie joyfully. She swept off her cap and her red hair came tumbling over her shoulders like a waterfall made of fire.

"Willie?" cried the king and queen in astonishment.

"Willie?" cried Brian and Elizar, equally astonished.

"Willie!" cried the knights and the pages, who were somewhat astonished, but mostly embarrassed.

"Yes, Father, it's me!" cried Willie as she ran to the king's arms.

Before he could ask her what had happened, a thunderclap split the air, and Grizelda came storming into the clearing. Her face was terrible to behold, and the knights shrank back from her in fear.

Taking one look at the dragon, Grizelda let out a mournful wail that shivered down the spines of all those present. But rather than raging at them for killing the dragon, she cried, "Where is Brian?"

Brian blinked in astonishment. "I'm here," he said, getting to his feet. "Why—"

"My son!" cried Grizelda. She ran to him and threw her arms around him.

"Son?" cried Brian in dismay.

"Yes," sniffed Grizelda. "My dear, long-lost son. I knew you by the dragon on your shoulder. I could stay away no longer."

"Dragon on his shoulder?" cried Elizar. "But *my* son had a dragon on his shoulder!"

Grizelda gasped. "Then . . ."

"Can it be?" cried Elizar.

"You're my father?" cried Brian. *"She's* my mother? *You're married?"*

"Elizar!" cried Grizelda joyfully.

"Maureen!" cried Elizar. "You changed your name!"

Grizelda rolled her eyes. "Maureen didn't fit my new image."

"But what happened?" asked Elizar. "When I came back from the war and found our cottage burned, I thought you were dead."

"No, no! I had left—because there was nothing left. I thought I had lost both of you. I thought the king had burned the cottage."

"Wait a minute!" cried King Mildred. "I remember the day we found Brian. We pulled him out of a cottage that had been set afire by a band of enemy soldiers we were trying to chase out of the country. I thought he was an orphan, so I brought him home to take care of him. That's how he got to be one of the pages."

"You mean you saved him?" screeched Grizelda. "Oh, what a fool I've been! All these years wasted on hate, on vengeance." She paused, then turned to the king. Dropping to her knees, she spread her arms and said, "I beg your forgiveness, Your Majesty."

The king looked at Willie. Then he turned to Grizelda and said, "Because of you, I nearly lost my daughter. Yet I now think that I would have lost her anyway—with less hope of ever getting her back. I will forgive you, my good woman— with the prayer that my own child will show the same mercy toward me."

Grizelda began to cry. With trembling fingers she touched her cheek. "Tears!" she said in astonishment. "I'm weeping!"

"There, there, my dear," said Elizar, patting her hand. "It's over now. We're together at last."

The king smiled. "And I would like to keep it that way. Elizar, will you—"

"Wait, Father," said Willie. "I have half a kingdom to run now, and I'm going to need some help. Let me, please."

Befuddled, the king turned to the queen. She smiled and nodded.

"All right, dear," he said, clearing his throat. "I guess you've earned that right."

Willie bowed to the king and said, "Thank you, Father. Elizar, will you be my chief of knights? For you are wise and kind—the truest signs of knighthood. In your heart you have always been a knight."

"With pleasure, if Maur . . . Grizel . . . *whoever!* . . . will come with me."

Grizelda grinned. "A thousand goons couldn't pull me away," she said, trying to pat her wild hair into place.

"Good," said Willie with a smile. Then she turned to Brian. Face stern, she pointed to the ground in front of her and said, "Please kneel here."

Brian swallowed nervously. Wondering if he was about to be punished for his statements about the royal family, he dropped to one knee before Princess Wilhelmina.

Placing her sword on his shoulder, Willie said, "Brian, I dub thee knight—for your courage, but even more for your compassion. For in turning from the dragon to help your friend, you gave up that which you desired most, as so often a true knight must. Now you have it back again. May great glory be yours."

And so it was. For in the days and years that followed, Brian carried out many daring missions for his father, the chief of knights, and their queen, Wilhelmina the Bold. The fox and the cat often accompanied him. Sometimes the bear came, too, though it mostly preferred to stay in Wilhelmina's castle, where it was fed more honey than was really good for it.

As for Willie herself, every once in a while, when duty allowed, she would set aside her crown and join Brian on one of his quests. And the adventures they had then were astonishing indeed.

About the Author and the Illustrator

BRUCE COVILLE was born in Syracuse, New York. He grew up in a rural area north of the city, around the corner from his grandparents' dairy farm. In the years before he was able to make his living full-time as a writer, Bruce was, among other things, a gravedigger, a toymaker, a magazine editor, and a door-to-door salesman. He loves reading, musical theater, and being outdoors.

In addition to more than seventy-five books for young readers, Bruce has written poems, plays, short stories, newspaper articles, thousands of letters, and several years' worth of journal entries.

Some of Bruce's best-known books are *My Teacher Is an Alien*, *Goblins in the Castle*, and *Aliens Ate My Homework*.

KATHERINE COVILLE is a self-taught artist who is known for her ability to combine finely detailed drawings with a deliciously wacky sense of humor. She is also a toymaker, specializing in creatures hitherto unseen on this planet. Her other collaborations with Bruce Coville include *The Monster's Ring*, *The Foolish Giant*, *Sarah's Unicorn*, *Goblins in the Castle*, *Aliens Ate My Homework*, and the *Space Brat* series.

The Covilles live in a brick house in Syracuse along with their youngest child, three cats, and a jet-powered Norwegian elkhound named Thor.

BRUCE COVILLE
Author of the SPACE BRAT series

WHO THROWS THE WORLD'S GREATEST TANTRUMS?

Imagine a planet called Splat where kids are raised by robots.
Now imagine a kid on that planet who has tantrums so awful
that he will be known across the gallaxy as Space Brat!

SPACE BRAT

SPACE BRAT 2:
BLORK'S EVIL TWIN

SPACE BRAT 3:
THE WRATH OF SQUAT

SPACE BRAT 4:
PLANET OF THE DIPS

SPACE BRAT 5:
THE SABER-TOOTHED POODNOOBIE

Published by Simon & Schuster

835-10

BRUCE COVILLE'S

The fascinating and hilarious adventures of the world's first purple sixth grader!

I WAS A SIXTH GRADE ALIEN

THE ATTACK OF THE TWO-INCH TEACHER

I LOST MY GRANDFATHER'S BRAIN

PEANUT BUTTER LOVERBOY

ZOMBIES OF THE SCIENCE FAIR

DON'T FRY MY VEEBLAX!

TOO MANY ALIENS

SNATCHED FROM EARTH

THERE'S AN ALIEN IN MY BACKPACK

THE REVOLT OF THE MINATURE MUTANTS

THERE'S AN ALIEN IN MY UNDERWEAR

FAREWELL TO EARTH

Bruce Coville's

Magic Shop Books

THE MONSTER'S RING
Russell is shocked when he finds out what can happen after three twists of the monster's ring.

JEREMY THATCHER, DRAGON HATCHER
She was just a little dragon. . . until she grew, and grew, and grew. . . .

JENNIFER MURDLEY'S TOAD
What do you do when your talking toad has an attitude?

THE SKULL OF TRUTH
It's talking, and it won't shut up!

Published by Simon & Schuster

What would you do if you discovered your teacher was from another planet?

Read all of Bruce Coville's bestselling series!